Meanwhile...
II

Kayleigh Hughes

For Mrs. Reilly, and my beloved dad, without whom, my passion for writing would not exist.

Thanks to Sonia, for your invaluable help with some of the finer details.

For Ms. Boylan.

CONTENTS

BOOK II

One

What was it that had made Caroline choose today to carry out this ordeal? Samuel hadn't taken his eye off the poor woman sitting by the toilet door. Was it the date - the anniversary of something? Some other occurrence on Caroline's way to work this morning? Had she stopped at the petrol station to fill up, only for the pump to be out of order? Or walked to work, carrying the gun and cable tie in her bag, just about turning up for work? If she did drive here this morning, maybe her car had broken down - like the Hungerford shooter Michael Ryan, in 1987 - and it changed her intended course of action. Maybe she had planned to do this tomorrow, but the supposed mishap this morning became the last straw. Maybe there wasn't a reason. There didn't always have to be with a suicidal person.

'How did you get here this morning,

Caroline?'

Gradually, Caroline turned from the door to Samuel. Looking how he probably did when Caroline had asked about his relationship with his wife.

'Did you walk?' Drive? Take the bus?'

'I ran.'

'Were you running late?'

Caroline brought her knees to her chin, wrapping her arms around her legs. The gun lay by her side. Had she forgotten about it? Her cradling whilst repeatedly mouthing 'Andrew' suggested just that. Even if Samuel made it out of here alive, Caroline may have not. That was the slow-biting reality that was beginning to manifest, like Samuel's mother's cancer. Samuel wanted Caroline to come out to the other side and be given the help she so desperately needed. Unfortunately, it was looking more and more to be an entirely different 'other side'.

'I ran.' Caroline eventually replied. 'Just ran.'

'Caroline?'

Samuel looked to the door as Buckley called.

'Caroline, what's going on in there?'

Should Samuel have tried to explain to Buckley? Tell everyone out there that they were likely going to have their work massively cut out for them?

'I don't think she can hear you.'

Samuel inhaled.

'What do you mean?'

How was he going to-

'I think she's too far gone. I don't…'

It didn't even sound good in Samuel's head.

'Does Caroline have the gun, Samuel?'

'No!'

Another lie. Why, you idiot, why? Attempting to save the poor woman who was probably beyond help? Samuel wouldn't know where to start trying to explain this to Harriet. Explain everything to her. Why he had fucked up so much in these twenty years, and awaited forgiveness that may never come this time. Harriet's deeply suppressed frustrations eating away at her, like the cancer that this idiot of a man's mother had succumbed to. What had Harriet seen in him?

'Can I try talking with Caroline again?'

Buckley's pause suggested he was thinking about it. Though probably wanting to say no.

'All right,' he replied. 'But anything-'

'I know, yeah.'

Samuel exhaled. It would only be for the worst, if things did change. His attention had been so focused on Caroline, he had only just begun to register his aching arm restrained by the cable tie. Because he never put himself first. Even his supervisor Rachel, he deemed more important. His children too, if he had any.

Maybe that was what Harriet saw in him. Their mutual nature of looking out for others - those in need. Looking for the best in others. Those like Caroline.

'Did you run away from Laura and Derek, Caroline?'

'It wasn't my fault.'

'What wasn't?'

Caroline's cradling grew faster. If Buckley could see her - if anyone on the other side could -

they'd stick her in a strait jacket and cart her away, like Percy Wetmore in *The Green Mile*. He had deserved it, though. Samuel didn't like to think such things about anyone, not even fictional people, whom, of course, you could wish to suffer hell on earth, and not await your comeuppance to knock on your front door.

'He knew.'

'Who knew, Caroline?'

'He knew, and he was going to…'

Caroline's buried her head in her arms. She inhaled. Then exhaled.

'He fucking knew.'

Maybe she wasn't referring to McNally this time. Was it Derek? Principal Glover? The boyfriend, Emmet? Did Caroline mean that 'he' knew about the school prank?

'Who, Caroline?'

Caroline kept her head down.

'Him.'

Samuel suppressed a sigh. Try as he might.

'Okay…what did he know?'

It came out slower than intended, in a way that could have suggested to Caroline that Samuel thought her to be an idiot - that word her friend Derek had called.

'You already know, Andrew.'

Samuel paused. Caroline had cornered him. He didn't... How did he respond to that? Stop himself going in more circles - stop himself potentially setting Caroline off again? Actually, the latter was probably quite unlikely. The cradling stopped.

'I told you already, Andrew,' Caroline said quietly, lifting her gun and pressing it under her chin. 'He didn't care.'

'About the prank?'

Jesus, you idiot - smart question, right there. Caroline's eyes began to well.

'Why didn't he care?' she said, tears streaming down her red cheeks. 'Why-'

'I care, Caroline.'

The under-bloody-statement of the century. But what Samuel hoped for to happen to Caroline at the end of all this, had long been crushed to dust, and he knew it. Gradually, Caroline's eyes met his.

'Why lie, Andrew?'

'I'm not.'

Caroline didn't take her eyes off Samuel.

'You care as much as they did.'

Samuel paused.

'What happened to them, Caroline? What happened to your friends?'

Samuel cared more than he could say. More than Caroline would likely ever know.

Two

17.2.91

Right, settle down, diary. It's gonna be a long one. That date was only two shakes short of a complete disaster. Emmet (more of an Evan to me) turned up dressed up like Crocodile Dundee, *and also realised our table hadn't actually been reserved. Went to McDonalds instead. Compromised on a box of McNuggets. Tasted like cardboard. Their shakes aren't much better. E must have taken his diet and exercise routine from the gospel of D, for he's thinner than a stick insect. Hm. Know I said it would be a long one, but I'm feeling embarrassed at the thought of telling you yesterday's antics. Basically, E asked about D, said to me 'is he free', like a certain Mr Humphries. Really hope he'll take no for an answer. Either D was being nosy, Arnold was too good for him, or he fancied an evening snack on*

our date night in McDonalds. Not really a date at this point, mind you, diary. Considering all of the above, I think I did well, considering I had only four hours sleep. Haven't yet told L, will do later. Maybe the milkshake kept me alert. Apparently four hours sleep is ideal for older people. No wonder the likes of Glover are on your arse like a shiny new set of razor sharp pins, the minute you enter them doors.

P Goss is apparently considering bringing his prank forward to April. If it isn't still snowing by then. Too confident for his own good. Just can't stop worrying about it. What if it backfires? Oh no, of course it won't, 'cause Goss'll have every nook and cranny worked out to the last. Or he thinks he will. Glover'll have him for beans on toast. Or do his own 'Jesus was nailed to the cross' with icicles, if word is caught before April.

Four hours later and still trying to reach the thousand word word-count on this HS&C. How is it so popular among our year group?

Still be worth it in the end, I suppose. Will go and see L and D later - unless I decide to watch

Dad's taped episode of Cheers.

Talk later, diary.

18.2.91

Damn it, forgot all about you, diary. Well, D and I rewatched TOTP. *Well, watched what we could before D's mother had several people (distant relatives, apparently) over and had us confined to his room. Asked about Saturday. D dismissed it as a coincidence, still chasing poor Arnold. Better than streaking, I suppose.*

L's beginning to share my apprehension about Goss' prank. Don't know why I'm calling it that, no one else is going to get it. He's never been very funny - maybe someone should get R. Lee Ermey on him. Christ, L somehow managed to walk into the wrong house last night. She's not going blind, is she? Trust it for the worst to plague my two best friends. I'd like to hope there wasn't alcohol involved, we're too close to exams for that. In a rare twist, Mum just left the next three night's dinner on the counter - Chinese menus, since Dad will be away 'for important business' and she just doesn't feel like

slaving over a scalding stove - not that I have any objection to making my own. The last time Dad took the leap of faith into cooking, he thought he could give Keith Floyd a run for his money. He may end up like Yootha Joyce (I cringe with sadness, diary). I don't know how Mum would handle it. All this shouting between them lately won't help. They don't want a divorce, do they?

20.2.91

Had beef in black bean sauce. Toilet will be my new best friend for god knows how long. Mum ate a few prawn crackers and disappeared into her and Dad's bedroom for the night. Will it be separation or divorce? Wonder if Dad's having a good time. May reread Misery.

Poor Dad, he's exhausted. Just as well he got a taxi home. At least no shouting, for now.

24.2.91

Can't sleep. Been like this the last couple of days. Too tired to write about it, though. Thank fuck I don't have school today. I'm not even going to start a sermon about how terrible Sundays are. The gospel according to Caroline

would be even worse than according to D. Thought about taking a walk. Maybe soon. Maybe not. Too cold, probably. The floorboards in this house are so old, my parents would be on my heels before I had even crossed the door.

Apparently, Thatcher only needed four hours sleep. No wonder she looked near decrepit by the end of her reign. My parents are only in their fifties, but look at them.

Never realised just how orange the streetlights actually are. Rather beautiful. My inability to sleep is no doubt thanks to that one and only Prat Goss.

Right, have put up with these sore and tired eyes long enough. Gonna try and get some kip. Later, diary.

Somehow, despite the snow-turned-to-ice neighbourhood, Marion Chambers from number sixteen went sleepwalking and nearly landed in a skip. When Dad catches word, he'll not let her hear the end of it, the poor woman.

L said sleepwalkers can be rather impressionable. Thank fuck Prat Goss doesn't

live within this vicinity.

Too many kids out being too fucking noisy. One of them will slip and fall then someone will curse the ever omnipotent powers above.

'I'll do whatever you want for twenty-four hours' is all one of them has been screaming for the last ten minutes. Along with actual screaming. At least I'm not hungover - speaking of such, I wonder how long Dad'll be nursing his for? If I ask that kid to smoke a joint or do cartwheels on the wall, I wonder would he? I bet not, but anything to shut them up.

Bad news for D - Arnold was spotted snogging his girlfriend of three weeks, tongues and all, outside that 'rotten bark lamb medallions' Indian, the other night.

Parsnips along with the usual roast tonight. Yuck. Neither L or D would touch them with a ten - no, twenty - foot barge pole. Wise, indeed.

26.2.91

Glover's been a right grumpy one these past two days. Many of the teachers have been stuck

in meetings with him. Some visibly scared shitless. Heard some teachers remark about his retirement. He'll definitely pass over the crown when this 'prank' happens. And it won't be icicles, it'll be Jesus' crucifixion MK II.

Lack of sleep made me write this:

The street lights project these people's lingering uncertainties

Prolonging their unending nights of troubling thoughts

The rain masks the unwarranted tears building up in their eyes

While the unyielding insomnia laughs at their full expense

The gradual morning sunrise never quite clears the fog

The amalgamating restlessness and fatigue, shaping the concrete shadow of their subconscious

The voices speak millions of sounds, to never be heard

I'm not trying to rip off Sound of Silence, *but in fairness, it's been in my head a lot recently. Don't know - in fact, don't think - Miss Ingram wouldn't like this poem if I showed it to her. Fuck, she'd throw me in with the school counsellor (called Audrey, apparently) for the next month. Maybe Audrey would encourage such expression. Really let rip. Actually, no, I'd have to eat more baked beans to do such a disgusting act. I don't need help, not in the way I've just written about, anyway.*

Wonder what Audrey would say about this 'prank'? Or my parents' shouting? Pre-prepared answers? 'How does that make you feel?' 'What are you thinking right now?' Or have I been watching too much TV? Not as much as L recently, anyway.

28.2.91

Shouting. Just shouting. No wonder I'm an insomniac. Just about reached the word count on H&SC.

So, the big day is the 15th April. Let's hope Glover's grumpiness has eased up by then.

Someone will let slip to him before then, I just know it. Then Prat Goss will get exactly what he fucking deserves.

Apparently Audrey's leaving at the end of the year. New career? Whatever it is, I wouldn't blame her for wanting to get out of this madhouse. Her room is only down the corridor from the 'plague room' - the classroom named so because it's where all the sick kids stem from; vomiting, sore throat, even the flu etc, etc.

I may think about seeing her.

Three

Samuel stood at the kitchen worktop, making himself a cup of tea. At last Thursday had arrived. So had an unusually long spell of warm and sunny weather. *Here Comes The Sun* had been this morning's alarm clock. At least it wasn't *Summer Holiday*.

Not even for Samuel's sake - the alarm clock wouldn't dared to have even squeaked again, once Harriet had smashed it to kingdom come. Harriet always had been more of the night owl, certainly in this relationship. It was the perfect accompaniment to being a nurse, or certainly working within that sector, anyway. Had Samuel's mum been like that, at all? Or did she have a good night's sleep, wake up at a reasonable hour bright eyed and bushy-tailed, ready to tackle the day's chores? If Dad was like that, he certainly never let on. Let on about the

countless sleepless nights he spent lying in that double bed, watching the empty pillow beside his, hoping for Mum to be there. Just once. From what Samuel could remember, his mum had looked mostly prim and proper, but not quite as far as a washing detergent advert. Although, according to a friend of hers, she could have done adverts on the radio, with her mellow voice, enticing even the most reluctant of spenders to cave in. Samuel drummed his fingers on his cup of tea. One which his mother probably made better than him. Cooking, beverages, they were always better when someone else made them. Mostly.

Samuel ought to do his laundry later, when today's big outing was over. To be honest, the laundry could have been done yesterday, or even the day before, but this was just typical of Samuel, of course. Leaving far too many things hanging off the threads of the absolute last minute. In hindsight, it was a wonder how Samuel had completed any of his schoolwork - coursework, especially - on time. Avoided many detentions. He remembered how a few other

fellow students were isolated for never handing homework in. Ivan Fulton lasted five weeks before Glover pegged and dished out his punishment, for that and other similar misdemeanours. Someone did once have their poetry assignment introduction accidentally misplaced by the slightly scatterbrained Mr Anderson, resulting in many tears and utter dismay. Some students just didn't care, or at least didn't seem to. And here Samuel was, soon to be heading off to university. What a strange place the world was.

Samuel poured the remaining tea down the sink, then headed upstairs to finally get dressed. Cynthia and Jude were probably doing the same, if they hadn't already. Samuel hoped Jude hadn't become *overexcited* about today - for Cynthia most likely didn't want a repeat of three Christmases ago. That was the last time a flashing fairy was the chosen ornament to top the tree. Though, unfortunately not the last time that Jude wet herself from her elation for her gifts, like the red toy fire truck when she was eleven.

Ah. As Samuel pulled a grey t-shirt over his

head, he smiled at the thought of it. Because he could. Jude always made things a little better – for him and Cynthia, which was all that mattered. Today, Samuel would simply walk past Ursula Olsen's house, ignore any of her usual, predictable, remarks. Unless Mr Olsen had decided to return.

No.

Chances of that happening weren't even paper thin. Cynthia had *rightfully* wondered how any sane individual would want to even stand in the same living room as Olsen. Apparently her kitchen (and skirtings, for that matter) were as dirty as her mouth. Surprise, surprise. Sometimes, though, Samuel wished that more people understood about Jude, and could accept her. Not the people in her street, per se, but in a broader sense. So there could be less bad - less evil, outright evil - in the world. Quite a long way to go for that. Samuel grabbed the nearest pair of shorts hanging over his chair. That was the sad and irrefutable truth. Maybe one day, though.

Boiling hot wouldn't even have been an

understatement, for yet another day in this endless heatwave. Not that it had bothered Jude, thanks to her favourite purple cap that had firmly shut out the bright sun from her eyes. Unfortunately, neither Samuel or Cynthia could say the same. Even Cynthia's pink linen dress hadn't fared too well in keeping her cool through today's great outing. As the three of them strolled through the bustling town centre, Jude slurped what remained of her ice cold orange drink – not enough to spill, if Jude happened to become particularly excited. It was only her fifth one too, along with a spot of lunch in a relatively new café called *Norman's*. Jude's choice: a generously sized BLT, bursting with extra juicy tomatoes and lashings of mayonnaise, with some of the tomatoes almost escaping onto Jude's plate before she gobbled them up. Samuel and Cynthia each tried a small carbonara dish, which wasn't bad, at all. Their server, Vic, had taken surprisingly well to Jude, treating her just the same as every other customer in the café – in fact, smiling that little bit more for Jude. Samuel noted how relieved Cynthia was by this, having left Vic a rather nice tip. Maybe Vic had a

background in helping those like Jude - worked a second job doing just that, maybe? Samuel particularly liked how even the most crowded of places never bothered Jude. In fact, it seemed to be yet another one of her innumerable fascinations. She had seemed to be particularly fixated on a balding middle aged man wearing a hat with a big sunflower attached, whistling his way alongside a row of shops. Cynthia placed her hand on Jude's shoulder, the other holding a bag of purchases for Jude.

'Be time to go home soon, Jude. Have some tea, if you fancy.'

Jude squeaked.

'Meatballs.'

'No, macaroni cheese tonight, Jude,' Cynthia corrected her. 'Some mushrooms too, if you want.'

'Mushy peas!'

'No, no,' Samuel said, letting out a chuckle. 'You had those last night. Little sliced mushrooms with your macaroni, tonight.'

'Mush'ooms..   Mush-mush-mushy-mush'ooms.'

Samuel and Cynthia exchanged another chuckle.

'You had fun today, Jude?' Samuel asked. 'Going to play with your new little fire truck and cars when you get back?'

Jude squeaked, bouncing up and down - nearly spilling her drink in the process - before Cynthia intervened.

'I don't want to be having to give you two baths tonight, Missy.'

Jude simply giggled.

'Ducks!'

Samuel smiled.

'You'll have your ducks, too.'

He looked to Cynthia.

'What time's the next train?'

'Fifteen minutes, I think.'

Samuel looked to the giggling young woman

beside him.

'What do you say, Jude? Home time?'

Jude nodded, squeaking with great elation.

'Home time! Home time!'

Home time, it was.

As the Biggerstaff's front door opened, Jude bound through down the hall and into the living room, giggling all the way. Cynthia and Samuel followed, albeit noticeably exhausted. Full of beans was Jude, and sometimes Samuel couldn't help wonder where it came from. Was it the Shredded Wheat and orange juice in the mornings? Her ham sandwiches at lunch? The macaroni cheese and sliced mushrooms she would be eating soon? Whatever it was, it would never stop being joyful for Samuel to watch. At least Jude always had a good night's sleep.

No sign of that Olsen woman, for once. In fact, it had seemed quieter than usual in her direction. The lady of the hour was firmly in a fire truck mood, so yet another viewing of her *Fireman Sam* tapes was likely to be on the cards.

Having volunteered to free Cynthia of her numerous bags stuffed with shopping, Samuel shut the door behind him with his free hand. He headed into the kitchen, just as Cynthia joined him.

'I'll help you pu-'

Cynthia shook her head.

'No, no,' she said, reaching into one of the bags. 'Better give this to Jude.'

Samuel nodded, taking the toy fire truck into the living room, to be greeted by that ever infectious grin.

Jude squeaked, clapping as she gazed upon her shiny new possession.

'Fire truck! Fire truck! Sammy got my fire truck!'

Samuel held it out, and found he couldn't stop himself smiling either, as Jude seized the fire truck and plonked herself on the carpet with it. Samuel stepped back. Always a joy.

'Is Sammy going to get a go with it too?' he

asked playfully.

'Yah!'

Jude began to push her truck back and forth.

Samuel chuckled, heading for the sofa, just as Cynthia entered.

'Dinner time in about thirty minutes, Jude. You can watch one of your tapes with it. What do you say, hm?'

Jude continued pushing her toy, making siren sounds. Cynthia approached the window blinds, pulling them open.

'Taps. Tap-taps.'

'No, no,' Cynthia replied, reaching in behind the television on the cabinet to switch it onto standby. Your video tapes, Jude. The taps are in the kitchen.'

Samuel placed his hands together on his knees, watching the woman on the carpet, rather contently playing with her fire truck.

'I bet I know which one you'd like, I *bet* I know.'

Still Jude's attention hadn't turned.

'When-he-hears-that-fire-bell-chime, Fireman-'

Jude shot up, giggling and clapping.

'Fireman Sammy! Fireman Sammy!'

Even Cynthia couldn't help chuckle.

Samuel nodded, once again sharing Jude's big smile. Cynthia headed for the door.

'Not until dinnertime, Jude,' she reminded the ever-ecstatic young woman. 'Just going to get changed, Samuel. Won't be long.'

Samuel nodded, and Cynthia disappeared upstairs.

Jude landed back on the carpet and reached for her truck, beginning to hum that same melody.

'You going to get changed at some point, too, Jude? I don't imagine you'd want us to have to peel those clothes off you?'

Jude shook her head, her tongue stuck far

out.

'Yucky, yucky!'

Samuel arose, and approached Jude, crouching before her.

'Sammy's go now?'

'Yah!'

Jude bounced up and retrieved another one of her fire trucks from her toy box in the corner, resuming that quite delightful humming.

It really had been particularly quiet next door without Olsen. Maybe someone had put her right. Or, again on the off-chance, perhaps this time she had been caught in the act, and had been escorted away by the police whilst the three of them had been out. It was a comforting thought, though only to a certain degree. Samuel just could not wish the worst on people. Even Ursula Olsen. Even the many murderers, paedophiles, and other abhorrences that occupied the world. He liked to think Cynthia was mutual on this matter (or just Olsen, in this case), but he had never been entirely sure. And didn't want to find

out. Throw nine years of trust - and probably the best friendship he would ever have - down the stinking drain. Why did he have to fuck things so often?

Footsteps sounded down the stairs and eventually into the kitchen. It had been a enjoyable day, but of course, Samuel would have to think about returning home soon. Despite that Cynthia made it crystal clear that he never did, Samuel didn't want to outstay his welcome. Even in a friendship as cherished as this one, he felt it was always on the brink of possibility. He would say one wrong thing, be banished from this house and street, and confined to spend his remaining days with Olsen.

Samuel cringed.

He turned, spying Cynthia at the door, in the corner of his eye.

'You can stay a bit longer, if you want,' she said softly. 'Even just to after dinnertime?'

'If you don't mi-'

'Of course not! I'll just get you some water.'

Samuel smiled and nodded. Jude's sixth orange juice drink of the day would accompany it, no doubt. The last thing either Samuel or Cynthia wanted was for Jude to become dehydrated - even in the slightest. Jude would be the first one to let you know if it was the case, in the same way that Bianca Henderson from down the road's Labrador, Cosmo, would firmly squash out any potential burglars, with his deep and deafening barks.

Samuel turned as Cynthia entered with a glass of water.

'Here you are.'

Samuel thanked her and took a sip.

'Dinnertime in five minutes, Jude. Samuel'll help you put out your table, and get your tape going, yeah?'

Jude squeaked, placing down her toy fire truck, and strode across to the other end of the living room, where her foldable table lay in the corner. As the two of them retrieved it, Samuel watched as Jude then placed it front of her special armchair. First class seating for the first

class young lady that was Jude Biggerstaff, without question.

'Now you just sit comfortably while I put Fireman Sam on for you,' Samuel said, heading for the television. As the screen flashed on, he opened the cabinet drawer to the usual array of multicoloured VHS boxes.

'Which one should we watch, hm?'

'Fireman Sammy!'

''Treasure Hunt' looks good, what about that one?'

'Yah! Treasure! Treasure!'

Samuel nodded, hearing Jude's claps of joy.

''Treasure Hunt' it is,' he said brightly, carefully pushing the tape into the machine.

Jude once again began to hum along to that ever catchy theme song. Samuel had been a little bit too old for this show himself when it had been originally broadcast, but he couldn't deny how good the theme song actually sounded. In fact, he could have said the same for many television

show themes of the eighties. That old Thames TV ident had always scared him, though, for some reason.

'*…hero-next-door.*'

Jude elicited a squeal. Samuel occasionally glanced at her, his heart warming as it always did when his best friend was like this.

'Think your dinner's almost ready, Jude. Macaroni and sliced mushrooms, yeah?'

'Mush'ooms! Mush'ooms!'

'And orange juice too, of course.'

'Yah!'

Jude's reply was as enthusiastic as before, but her attention was solely focused on Fireman Sam. Samuel took another sip of water, and watched along with Jude. Sam and his colleague, Elvis, effortlessly slid down the poles and hurried to their fire engine. Hopefully not to be stopped by-

'Dinnertime, Jude.'

Cynthia entered, holding a medium-sized

plate of macaroni and mushroom slices in one hand, and cutlery in the other. Jude sat upright, eyeing the plate as Cynthia placed it on the table.

'Mush'ooms! Mush'ooms! Mush'ooms!'

'I'll be back with your orange juice, in a moment, Missy.'

Jude lifted her fork and stabbed it into a couple of pasta shells, gradually bringing it into her mouth, and began to chew. And again. And again. Cynthia entered with a blue beaker full with Jude's favourite beverage.

'Remember to wash it down with your juice,' Cynthia said, placing it into the table's cup holder.

Jude nodded, munching away, still immersed in *Fireman Sam.*

Cynthia at last settled on the sofa adjacent to Samuel's, exhaling. With relief, and much exhaustion, at a guess.

'I'll have something a bit later, probably when Jude's gone to bed.'

Samuel nodded.

'Are you sure you don't want anything, even a sandwich?'

'Ah no, honestly, I'm fine, Cynthia,' Samuel smiled, shaking his head. 'Thank you for today, though.'

Cynthia reciprocated his smile.

'Do you know, I really quite enjoyed it myself. Not as much as our Lady Muck over there, mind you.'

Samuel chuckled. Their Lady Muck. Jude was making good headway with her meal, but that was only to be expected. There would never be seconds with Jude around. Cynthia sat up a little straighter.

'Pretty quiet next door,' she remarked. 'Off on holiday again, no doubt. Good riddance. Will give my head peace.'

Give *everyone* peace, for that matter.

Samuel looked back to the television. The tape must have been about halfway through, or

thereabouts.

'Is your pasta tasty, then, Jude?'

Samuel turned to her. No reply. The plate was still half full, but Jude hadn't moved.

'Jude?'

Cynthia looked too.

'Jude?'

A mushy mix of orange, green, and brown, exploded from Jude's mouth. Her head leaned back, as low moaning sounded from her vomit-filled mouth. Her eyes rolled back, while her arms and legs began to jerk.

Cynthia shot up, as Samuel gradually felt his way from the sofa, eyes fixated on what was unfolding before him.

'Jude, oh God, Jude!' Cynthia cried, rushing over to her. 'Jude, please-'

She held onto her daughter, her eyes beginning to water.

'Ambulance. Call for an ambulance,

Samuel.'

It was quiet, but completed panicked. Samuel nodded, and stumbled out of the room to the landline, just about bringing himself to do so. As he asked for that all too urgent ambulance, Samuel watched as Cynthia held her daughter, feeling every fibre of distress and more, that was clearly running through the tearful lady's body. Samuel breathed in and out, waiting until help arrived. It was all he *could* do.

Four

Moylan had thought about the day ahead of him. The students, the parents that would accompany each one during the parent-teacher meetings, this afternoon. Whether he would have another brush with Scanlon, or delightful chat with Helen. Talk about yet another trip she had with her young daughters, Millie and Dorothy. Perhaps Moylan would have the pleasure of meeting them one day. Maybe Millie and Dorothy would be in the car with their father, waiting for Helen to eventually collapse into the front passenger seat, up after a long and strenuous day. Such a shame she wasn't here beside Moylan in his car, right now. She would also adore this radio station's song choice. *It's Raining Men*. Indeed it would be, later on.

Helen had been talking about transferring to an all girls grammar school, next term. That was

what Moylan had overheard, anyway. She must have been waiting until the right moment to tell him. Or Scanlon, who would no doubt be begging her until her wit's end not to leave. Utterly dire was Scanlon. Perhaps Helen's replacement would be a young, male, newly qualified teacher. Oh, yes. Moylan would certainly make him feel welcome. By pure luck, he could still be learning to drive. He wouldn't say no to a lift in the mornings. Or to anything.

What a long and strenuous afternoon, that was not. Moylan could feel his mouth almost curling into a perfect Cheshire Cat grin, as he sat in his car. Most other staff had now since gone home. Moylan needed to wait. The shoe box lay tucked away under the front passenger seat.

Such satisfaction he'd felt greeting each boy and their parents, and divulging his wisdom and ever sincere praise to them. Ritchie Keenan was the first. Moylan would speak to him first thing tomorrow morning. Just about the few improvements his coursework needed. Helen had seemed relaxed during hers. Was she sure about this transfer? More than what Moylan was

about the box, perhaps. She couldn't know. Moylan had kept the box in here, just in case. Did Scanlon know? Those toilet breaks he had taken, could he have used them to do the worst? Had Gavin Woods opened that mouth of his to Helen and Scanlon about the shoes? Yes, that's what was in it. All of that running was going to be worth it.

Five

Samuel stared at the toilet door. There hadn't been anything from Buckley for a while. He wanted to burst in and snatch that gun from Caroline, didn't he? Because he knew that Samuel had lied. Or because he knew he would have been able to do so without Caroline noticing, and take full advantage of her utter shell of a state of mind. Samuel almost wished that Buckley would say more than he had been during this entire ordeal. More than those...phrases? Something that might just make Caroline see the light. Free her from the clutches of Andrew McNally.

If only.

Samuel's hopefulness, his desire for what was right...it wasn't possible. It cursed him just like his damned anticipation of Harriet's forgiveness. Wanting the best for people - why

did it have to be such a…

Samuel bowed his head, just like Caroline's was. Such a…

Shit. He couldn't say what-

'I didn't run, I took the bus.'

Samuel looked at Caroline. The gun was still by her side. Her voice, it was silly. Childish.

'They wouldn't let me drive,' Caroline continued. 'So I ran for it.'

'For the bus?'

'No, no. Away from them, silly.'

It was childishness that would have been adorable if Jude had said it. This, however, wasn't even unnerving. The creepiest of creepy horror films looked tame compared to it.

'He wasn't going to catch me. Child-snatcher wasn't gon' catch…'

Did Caroline mean Glover? McNally? Her friend Derek? Or seemingly no longer her friend. Was that what she had meant when talking about

Laura and Derek?

This prank?

'Who's that, Caroline?'

'Couldn't catch me…you couldn't catch me, Andrew.'

The southern drawl had resurfaced, coupled with the child-like tone.

What was Buckley making of this? He was only pretending to understand - he may as well have screamed it through a bull horn at its loudest setting. McNally was laughing - full on chortling. Sipping that ice cold glass of brandy. Peter Moylan - Joan's brother - if he and McNally had met in another world, they would be sharing a pint - not of brandy - but the prolonged tears of Caroline Cleaver. Chanting for her to do it. Pull the trigger. Bask in their filthy, rotten, gut-covered victory. A world where the lights were permanently broken. Full of sinkholes. Full of…

Samuel cringed. Jude, think of Jude. That radiant smile. Bubbly demeanour. Those ever

excited squeaks. The Spice Girls - internally, Samuel could almost feel himself chuckling. But he couldn't. Caroline. Harriet. Joan. Even McNally. They were all pecking at his mind. Samuel may never have laughed again. Like Caroline. She hadn't known what it was like to laugh for so long. Unlike Samuel, she never would. He looked at the woman sitting by the door. Holding the gun. Not aiming it, instead keeping it by her side.

'Why do you git the windaw seet?'

Samuel glanced to the radiator alongside him. Window?

'Why daws the ther'pist awways git the windaw seet?'

Her drawl was growing thicker and thicker. And becoming as hard to make out as Ursula Olsen's.

'Awways the windaw seet in this offuce.'

This wasn't…oh.

Too far gone was now an understatement. What was this? What could Samuel call it? It was

like something out of a film. Psychosis? What would his supervisor Rachel have said? What would she have said about all of this - whatever the hell it was? What would she have done? Kept Samuel on track about what to do? Tried to talk with Caroline, herself? If she was in Samuel's place, this would have been over in five minutes. Rachel had had to deal with two suicide attempts just last week, so it would have been child's play. Caroline would have made it out, Buckley could have stopped the pretending that he wouldn't have been doing in the first place, and Samuel could have given his undivided attention to Joan, during their intended session in his office. Could have been. If Samuel just…

He suppressed a sigh. Was Rachel watching the news? Feeling as distressed - *panicked* - as Harriet had? You idiot, of course she was.

'Three bullets. That's all I have.'

It was quiet and detached, again.

'Caroline?' Buckley called. 'Do you have the gun, or does Samuel?'

Caroline stared at the floor.

'Caroline?'

'It's by her side.'

Said all too like Caroline. Maybe Buckley hadn't heard him - Samuel had had to shout all of the other times. For once, his fingers were crossed that-

'The gun's by her side?'

Damn it.

Samuel glanced between the door and Caroline.

'Yeah, but she's not using it. Just holding it.'

Caroline could, though. Samuel and Buckley both knew that. That was where Buckley couldn't pretend.

'Only three. Not six.'

'Caroline?'

She didn't flinch at Buckley's voice. 'Caroline,' Buckley continued. 'How about giving the gun to Samuel? For good, this time. Hm?'

Caroline squeezed her hand around its handle.

'Three bullets. You can't have them, Andrew.'

She began to shuffle her feet. Was Caroline trying to soothe herself?

'Samuel, I'm sorry that I didn't ask this before now, but has Caroline restricted you in any way – your arms, or anything?'

Samuel glanced at his aching arm. It did seem strange that Buckley hadn't enquired about it until now.

'Yeah, my hand's secured to the pipes with a cable tie.'

'That's it, nothing else?'

'No.'

Samuel could also sense Buckley nodding.

'What do you say, Caroline?' Buckley asked. 'How about doing that for me?' Give Sam-'

'I fucking heard you the fucking first time.'

It was said like a grumpy teenager. No. Like Edward Norton in *Primal Fear,* when his other personality emerged. Or both. Whichever one it did resemble, it had certainly startled Samuel. Buckley too, no doubt. This wasn't a personality shift, though. Caroline didn't mean any of it. She probably would have said it herself, if she wasn't stuck in this…whatever this bloody was.

'And I ain't fucking doing it.'

Samuel looked warily at Caroline. Better tread carefully, again.

'Don't you fucking make me, Andrew. Don't fucking make me jump out the fucking window.'

'I won't, Caroline.'

'I ain't doing it.'

Samuel nodded, trying to show the assurance that Caroline would probably never acknowledge.

'That's okay.'

Neither would have…oh, did it need saying?

'That's good to hear, Caroline.'

Samuel looked to the door, as Buckley responded. Still pretending? Or beginning to genuinely understand? Even if Buckley did, it would only be surface-level.

Samuel turned to the woman by the door, squeezing the gun.

'Will you do it for me, Caroline? Do it for Samuel?'

Six

Samuel couldn't remember the last time he had been in a hospital. In any capacity. Not even if he had gone to see his mother, when she was on her last legs from her cancer. His father didn't seem to want to trouble Samuel with it. He would mention things here and there, but all with that ever familiar vagueness. In fairness, what parent would would want their child to see the other in such a terrible state? Distressing state. Almost as much, if not *as* much, as the sight before him and Cynthia. Maybe this *was* more distressing because Samuel was actually here to see it. Still in her clothes from earlier, Jude had finally calmed down, now lying in a hospital bed. The paramedics had been brilliant, doing what they had to do. Doing a hell of a better job at keeping Cynthia level-headed than the sorry excuse that Samuel had made. They had asked a lot of

questions - if it was her first, any allergies, was she diabetic - all necessary, he took it. Jude had been taken straight to the emergency department - probably because it hadn't happened before. Something about a seizure. Samuel hadn't known much about them. Only of epilepsy. Not the ins and outs, though. Just what he had seen on television, which was probably far from reliable or accurate.

Jude had been looking between Samuel and a rather teary-eyed Cynthia, but only that.

Cynthia was probably also longing for some sort of sound that wasn't a beeping monitor, or the hum of staff and patient conversations. Or even a yawn from the notably sleepy Jude.

What would Samuel tell Harriet? Given this place was where she would end up working, she wouldn't be too pissed off at him for missing tonight, would she? She would understand - well, she would have to, anyway. Harriet seemed to be fascinated about Jude, even though the two of them had never set eyes on each other. Maybe she wouldn't adore Jude like how Samuel did,

but there was no way Harriet would detest her. She may have been a bit overwhelmed with Fireman Sam and the fire trucks, though.

Samuel watched as Cynthia stroked Jude's head.

'Oh, Jude,' she said, exhaling softly. 'What's happened to you, eh?'

Another precious moment, which Samuel did not want to fuck up. Not this time.

A short and stocky, balding, dark-skinned man with a clipboard appeared. At a guess, the long-awaited doctor. Cynthia sat up, finally shifting her attention to him.

'Sorry to keep you waiting,' he began. 'I'm Doctor Bhatti. So Jude has had a seizure, hm?'

Cynthia said nothing.

'That's what the paramedics told us.'

Doctor Bhatti nodded.

'I'm going to refer Jude for a EEG scan, up at neurology in a few days. That way we can check for any abnormal brain activity - apart

from the learning difficulty, of course. And for the possibility of epilepsy.'

Cynthia looked between Jude and Doctor Bhatti, fighting to stop more tears escaping.

'Epilepsy? Do you mean-'

'Not to worry, Mrs Biggerstaff. There is medication that can be prescribed to treat the seizures.'

'Would it stop them?'

'That depends. It's different for everyone.'

Cynthia looked over the motionless young woman.

'Along with the blood tests,' Doctor Bhatti continued. 'I would like to examine Jude's reflexes and mental function, if that is all right?'

Cynthia paused, not looking as if she was taking one bit of any of this in. She gradually looked to Samuel, who placed his hand on her shoulder. Cynthia sniffed.

'Okay.'

Doctor Bhatti nodded.

'All right. I think, given this is her first seizure, that Jude should be kept in overnight for observation. Just in case.'

Samuel briefly rubbed his hand across her shoulder. It was the best he could do.

'Do you mean it'll happen again?'

'Not always. She could have only this one and that'd be it.'

Cynthia lowered her head.

'I know they can be terribly frightening to watch, Mrs Biggerstaff. But I assure you, we will look after her the best we can. With plenty of rest and fluids, she should be back to normal by tomorrow, and can be discharged.'

As Samuel and Cynthia stepped out of the taxi, Cynthia kept her head low. Eleven o'clock. But the late hour didn't seem to matter. Not even that there had been just enough change between them both for the fare. Samuel could only apologise, but the driver shrugged it off, and drove away. He offered to put his arm around

her, as they headed for the front door. A better comfort than what would have been contrived platitudes. Samuel glanced at Olsen's house. Still not a peep. Not even when the ambulance had arrived. They entered, Samuel shutting the door behind them. Cynthia lead the way into the living room, sat in Jude's chair, putting her head in her hand.

'Oh, Samuel, I'm sorry. I shouldn't…'

Samuel sat down on the sofa next to her, almost mirroring how he and Jude had done so earlier. Cynthia's red-rimmed eyes were painful to see, but not as painful as it was to think about Jude. Or to see her so quiet. So still. Not shouting with joy about her red fire truck. Or beating Samuel yet again at another game of snooker.

Samuel struggled to speak, almost as much as the woman beside him. Sleep wasn't likely to be either one's friend, for this long and horrible end to a horrible day. Even if it had just been a seizure, nothing could describe how Samuel felt about it – and certainly not Cynthia. Have one seizure but never another. Presently, that was

what stuck in Samuel's mind. A freak occurrence, not to be seen or talked of again? That was the only comfort Samuel could give himself about it. Bloody hell, what kind of...

Oh, Jude.

At last, Cynthia released her head from her hand and leaned back, sighing. Her eyes darted around.

'Oh, I don't know.'

She exhaled.

'Tomorrow. Tomorrow. Tomorrow.'

Cynthia moved onto her side, firmly grasping the chair's leather arm.

And exhaled.

Samuel lay in his bed, staring at his bedroom light. Switched off, of course. How he had tried to catch even an hour of rest. Instead an unusual cold feeling had lurked with him as the hours had ticked away. A feeling that was supposed to be pleasant during this time of year. It had only been a seizure, but it was a seizure. Something most

people were unprepared for. That, sometimes the sufferers of the seizures, themselves, couldn't deal with. Wasn't that what attributed to Ian Curtis' demise? Cynthia, how was she? Still sitting in Jude's chair? Sleeping with the light on? Crying some more? Doctor Bhatti did assure her and Samuel that seizures weren't life-threatening. Why did they have to look so bloody frightening, then? As a heart attack. Or a stroke. Or something which Samuel couldn't even curse upon Olsen. He turned to his bedside clock. Two minutes to five. Samuel hated the fact that he could worry ultimately all for nothing, sometimes. It was common at his age, apparently. That's what his neighbour Lynn said, anyway. Maybe it would stop when Samuel reached his thirties. A lot of things would stop, perhaps. His disorganised room. Instead of grunts and shrugs, maybe his dad would actually sit down and explain everything - not when Samuel was thirty, of course. His dad would likely be six feet under by then. Samuel looked to the window, as the sunrise began to emerge. Maybe it was all for nothing. He shut his eyes, hoping this time to nod off.

'Oh, Samuel, I just couldn't sleep.'

Cynthia had barely managed to finish her usual morning coffee, before they left for the hospital. The same beeping monitors and hum of conversations droned endlessly in Samuel and Cynthia's ears, as a nurse lead them to Jude's ward.

'Nor me. It was awful.'

Whether his words were reassuring or not, it was better that he had made *some* effort this time. Would words - these, or any that he would speak - show that Samuel felt Cynthia's anguish? What would him using words rather than actions this time, show?

Samuel made several glances at the beds they passed. Cynthia was keeping her gaze straight ahead, no doubt. It didn't need saying what mattered the most to her right now.

'Oh, Jude.'

The three of them approached the last bed. The young woman was sitting upright, with a half-full bowl of mushy cornflakes and spoon

placed before her on her table. She was the only one between the three of them to have had her beauty sleep. Cynthia headed beside Jude, wrapping her arms around her. Much of Cynthia's distress seemed to relieve itself as she savoured this precious moment. Samuel allowed a little smile to break out.

'Did you enjoy your cornflakes, Jude? Not as much as your Shredded Wheat, I bet.'

Jude nodded, albeit rather slowly.

'Fortunately, there haven't been any more seizures, and Jude seems to have recovered well enough,' the nurse began, as Cynthia finally let her daughter go. 'Just remind me, who was her doctor?'

'Doctor Bhatti,' Cynthia replied.

'He should be round very soon, to talk with you, and probably discharge her.'

Cynthia nodded.

'If you need anything, just give one of us nurses a shout, all right?'

'Okay, thank you.'

The nurse turned away, and they both looked at the young woman in the bed. The quiet young woman. It must have taken quite a lot out of Jude. Not too much, hopefully.

As the three of them walked up the Biggerstaff's driveway to the front door, Cynthia and Samuel found that Jude had to held by the arms. It wasn't that her balance was uneven, instead the notable lack of energy. No 'Sammy', or even one of her squeaks. Just gurgling like a baby, in its place. Wait until the EEG, was all the doctor said. As if Cynthia hadn't waited long enough last night. Maybe the doctor had been right about Jude's recovery, though. Maybe because of her learning difficulty, it would take that little bit longer. Cynthia likely wanted to have the same mindset, but couldn't.

Still no sound from Olsen's house. In this instance, thank bloody Christ.

They entered into the hallway, and gradually into the living room.

'Let's sit you down over here,' Cynthia said

softly, as they approached Jude's chair, and helped her sit down. Jude looked between them both, sticking out her tongue.

'Are you thirsty? You want some orange juice?'

Nothing. Except for her tongue.

'Or what about some more sleep?' Cynthia continued. 'I bet you're knackered, eh?'

Jude gurgled, her tongue still stuck out.

'Come on,' Cynthia said brightly. 'Bedtime for you.'

Rather than springing up in her usual stride, Jude rose from the chair bit by bit. Should Samuel have stayed, or headed on? Wait until Cynthia said something? He watched as they exited the living room and headed for the stairs.

'Hold on to the bannister, Jude. That's it.'

Samuel moved out into the hallway, as they continued up.

'Just have to brush your teeth and put your jammies on, and then we can start…'

Should Samuel have left? Gone and sat back on the sofa? For now, he simply leaned against the wall behind him. Maybe Cynthia would have preferred to be left alone for the next few days. Even to get her head around all of this. He couldn't blame her if that was the case. Samuel listened to the footsteps upstairs. Finally going into Jude's room? It seemed so, as Cynthia eventually came down the stairs.

'Fast asleep.'

She said it not even in a whisper, though it was pretty unlikely to wake Jude. Cynthia approached Samuel, placing her hand on his arm.

'A few days, Samuel,' she sniffed. 'A few days, and maybe…'

Cynthia exhaled.

Samuel knew what she meant. Oh, he knew.

He didn't know how to tell her, though.

It was over. The EEG was done. Along with numerous other tests. Cynthia said she had never answered as many questions about anything as this. Then again, if it was all necessary…

Since then, it had been forty-eight hours of waiting. How had Cynthia coped with it? Oh, snap out of it, Samuel. She hadn't. Every hour - no, every second - that had passed, she could not bear. As much as - in fact, more - than Samuel. Those sleep-deprived nights seemed to finally be catching up with him. He lay on the sofa in the living room, struggling to keep his eyes open. At eleven in the morning. No doubt, Cynthia had still been the polar opposite. She had eaten - which was something, at least. By this afternoon she would know the results. Jude was moving around on her own again. Playing with her fire trucks. A full bowl of Shredded Wheat had been consumed on both mornings, along with her usual lunch and dinner. All of that rest had been worth it, it seemed. Maybe the seizure on Thursday had just been a blip. It would blow over, and he would have been worrying for nothing. Something, which if it were an Olympic sport, Samuel would walk away with the gold. Samuel yawned. It wouldn't even matter if his dad was here, if he did fall asleep. His dad would possibly join him, when he came home later tonight. Harriet, not so much. She longed to hear

more about Jude. Prompted him to stay over tonight. By then, maybe he wouldn't have much to tell Harriet. And catch up on his sleep properly this time.

Perhaps Harriet and Jude could finally meet. And Cynthia, of course. Harriet could do what Samuel should have done from the offset. Comfort her. Not potentially fuck it up. Some people were just destined to follow a certain path in life - whether a personal or career one. Harriet was made for hers, in a way that someone could have a talent for something, whether they liked it or not. At one point, a younger Cynthia had a desire to be a primary school teacher - and then Jude came along. Lovely Jude.

Ring, ring.

Samuel gradually opened his eyes.

Bugger. He had only-

Three-thirty. Bloody hell, what if-

Ring, ring.

Samuel peeled himself from the sofa, staggering out to the telephone, slightly bleary-

eyed.

'Hello?'

'Samuel?'

Cynthia's voice was quiet.

'Oh, God, Samuel….they said…something in the brain…some sort of…sort of tumour.'

Samuel froze. He couldn't…

'Cynthia, where are you? Are you at home?'

Cynthia let out a loud sob.

'Oh, Samuel…'

He didn't-

'Hold on, Cynthia. Hold on.'

Neither Cynthia or Samuel had quite grasped it yet. They sat on opposite sofas in the living room, mostly in silence. There were many big words that Cynthia didn't understand. The oncologist had said one thing that she did understand, but didn't want to accept.

'Inoperable. He said-'

She reached into her handbag by her feet, producing a notebook.

'-''Glio…Glioblastoma. Deep in the brain''.'

She set it down.

'He said because of where it is, it's too risky to remove it. I don't…'

Cynthia put her hand to her mouth.

'What happens now? What about treatment?'

Cynthia lifted the notebook.

'''Put her on keppra'', along…along with another one, both for the epilepsy. I have to keep her here, except…except for the chemo.'

Samuel nodded. He understood, but he didn't. Why it had to be Jude. This young woman with the most infectious grin and endearing squeaks.

'Just be looking after her as I usually do, I suppose.'

Samuel watched Cynthia fidgeting with the notebook. Breathing in and out. In and out.

'This is what my daughter gets? For having someone that loves her? Someone that… She gets this?'

Samuel had no words. None at all. He was wondering the same thing.

He could have asked why a million and one times. Jude was upstairs, unaware her mother and Samuel were having this conversation. It wasn't even that. Indeed, Samuel had many more questions, but found that all he could do was listen.

'Is it all right to go up and see Jude?'

Cynthia nodded.

'Of course, of course.'

Samuel acknowledged it with some attempt at a smile, then headed upstairs.

As he climbed the stairs, Samuel felt almost as if he wanted to turn back. Away from this. Turn back and see Jude bound up these stairs.

Hear her joyfully call 'Sammy!'.

Samuel turned the corner to a door, showcasing Jude's name in multicoloured letters. He knocked it gently, and then pushed. Jude's room was covered with red and purple striped wallpaper, two chest of drawers and cabinet. Lots of snooker, *Fireman Sam*, and *Danger Mouse* decorated the rest of her room. The young woman was on the carpeted floor, pushing a fire truck at snail's pace.

'Hello, Jude,' Samuel said brightly, crouching down before her. 'You having fun?'

Jude pushed it once more, then gradually nodded.

'Can I play too?'

'Y…Yah.'

That was it. How did he respond?

'S…Pl…'

They were low noises - not even words. Samuel stood up, and headed for the door. Hesitantly, but urgently. With all his might, he

fought not to rush out and slam it behind him. As Samuel made his way downstairs, he suppressed several sighs, gripping the bannister.

He had to go. Just had…to go.

The empty house was empty no longer. Samuel looked blankly at the television, only vaguely registering the chink of Harriet's spoon stirring their tea. Or the ever messy living room. It wasn't even an inkling of compensation for their missed night on Thursday. Harriet insisted that it didn't matter. Because it was the first time? Because of Jude? Samuel sat up, as Harriet entered with two mugs, and joined him on the sofa.

'Maybe give it a few days, Samuel. You need your sleep, you can't-'

'I know, I know,' he said, exhaling. 'I know. Cynthia. What…What should I do for her?'

Samuel caught her look, as she put her arm around him.

'What you've already been doing.'

Samuel looked to the television. What had

he been doing, exactly?

'It might just be enough.'

Or worth nothing at all. Nothing.

Two days later, Samuel felt ready. All the courage he wished he possessed, he had spent these last two long days mustering it up inside him. He just needed a clean pair of jeans to put on, and then head over. Samuel felt ready to face what he had basically run away from two days ago. How could he? All this annoyance and frustration, and Jude wouldn't even be aware. Sitting in silence, saying nothing? That wasn't what Harriet meant by what would be enough, did she? Samuel would say something this time. He would. Make sure Cynthia knew he was listening. That he was as good the friend Cynthia had claimed. Samuel pulled his jeans up over his waist. Now to-

Maybe he could leave it another day. Or two. So as not to overcrowd Cynthia and Jude. Two more days and he would be ready.

'Come on in, Samuel.'

Samuel exchanged a smile with the visibly worn-out Cynthia, as he stepped into the hallway, out of the pelting rain. As he removed his saturated coat, Cynthia took it and hung it over the nearest radiator. Her smile seemed only a burden for her. Samuel followed Cynthia into the living room.

'How's Jude doing?'

Cynthia sat down in Jude's chair, and sighed.

'Not too good,' Cynthia began. 'I can get her up and down the stairs all right, but not into the bathroom. She just won't go.'

Samuel nodded. He didn't want to, though.

'Had another seizure last night. She's just in bed.'

And her first bit of chemotherapy yesterday.

Once again, Samuel didn't know what to say. For fuck's sake.

'I don't know if you'd want to see her, she's not…'

He did. It wasn't going to be a repeat of last

time. Samuel would make sure of that.

'Jude's my friend. Of course I do.'

Cynthia paused, then gave what must have been her hardest smile yet.

'Okay.'

Samuel felt himself grip the bannister as he reached the landing, though not as tightly as before. How much worse would Jude be? Sleeping? Samuel opened the door, to see Jude lying across her bed in her pyjamas. Her face. Pale. Bloated. Like the rest of her body. Samuel walked over to her.

'Hi, Jude.'

Low moaning sounded.

'You tired? All that moving around the house today, hm?'

The moaning sounded a bit louder.

'What about your fire trucks? Still playing with those?'

Jude wasn't looking at him, rather up at the

ceiling. The moaning grew even louder.

'What is it? You need the toilet?'

And louder. Samuel reached out his hand to her arm.

'I'll just help you si-'

Jude didn't budge. Or rather couldn't.

'Cynthia!'

Samuel headed out into the landing.

'Cynthia!

She rushed up the stairs faster than what Jude would ever do now.

'She can't seem to move. I thought she maybe-'

Cynthia made her way downstairs again, rushing to phone for help. Was it adrenaline causing her to do it herself, this time?

What could it be this time? What could it *possibly* be?

'I'm very sorry, Mrs Biggerstaff. Another tumour has been located in Jude's spinal cord.'

Cynthia had looked at the middle-aged oncologist, Doctor Sarah Ford, whilst holding Samuel's hand - which she could have done as tightly as she wanted.

'It's highly likely that Jude will have to spend her remaining time in the hospital ward, unfortunately, due to the high possibility of paralysis from the tumour, and likelihood of it recurring.'

It was probably all that Cynthia had been able to register of this earlier conversation. Three, maybe four, months. That's what they were giving Jude. Even with chemotherapy and medication. Even with the best care they could offer. Samuel and Cynthia hadn't even made it to the hospital exit, when Cynthia finally let it all out, and cried and cried into Samuel's shoulder, until nothing more could come out.

Samuel couldn't go home just yet. He couldn't leave Cynthia. She had had enough people do that. For God's sake, why did he nearly run from Jude, the other day? Because he was young, and like most people his age, wasn't

expected to understand? At some point, Samuel had to say goodbye. In eighteen years of being, how had he never done that? Not even to his own mother. What about Cynthia? He didn't believe this would be her first goodbye. Her own parents, grandparents, and other relatives, maybe. With no fewer amount of tears and anguish. Or every little pinprick of whatever she was feeling about her daughter. Eighteen years-old, just like Samuel. The one question that rolled around in his mind, was no doubt exactly what Cynthia wondered too. Now she wouldn't even be able to wake up tomorrow morning and hear Jude stomping down the stairs - 'Breakfast! Breakfast!' - the same way as when it was Christmas, or her birthday.

Samuel sighed. Jude's birthday. Just this past April.

As Samuel followed behind Cynthia into her house, he made sure to give her enough space. This time, she didn't even remove her jacket, and sat down on the stairs. Her look - was it distress? Frustration? Something else entirely?

'What kind of mother must I be?'

Cynthia put her head in her hands, almost looking as if she might start ripping it out.

'To have let Ursula Olsen just keep getting away with it. To keep-'

Cynthia inhaled heavily, eventually releasing her hands. Her face was set. For the first time, Samuel could see an emotion she had clearly always tried her best to conceal from him. A cloud of red gathered in her eyes.

'Jude's been living on borrowed time, is that what they were trying to tell me? That it wouldn't matter as much, because she was 'different'?'

Samuel wanted to tell Cynthia 'no'. Different to any onlooker out there, maybe. But, why should there have been anything wrong with being different? Why did it have to provoke such vitriol? Cynthia looked up at Samuel, the mist seeming to have cleared.

'What am I supposed to do? What am I meant to tell myself?'

What was *he* meant to tell Cynthia? Not that it would be all right - the child was never supposed to go first. Certainly not Jude.

'I won't even be able to give my daughter a proper goodbye,' Cynthia continued. 'I could be there until she goes, but…'

Samuel sat down next to her, and put her arm around her shoulder. It might have been enough. But it wouldn't be. Nothing would be.

Samuel's sheets had become as creased as linen trousers, with the endless tossing and turning he inflicted on himself each night. He was counting each hour of each day carefully. Samuel had even offered to talk with Cynthia every few days on the phone. To try and comfort her. Give her something. Each day was horribly long, and ten times that for Cynthia. Three months had passed. The tumour was bigger than a golf ball. Jude hadn't uttered a word during the numerous times Samuel and Cynthia saw her in the hospital. Nor had she moved at all on her left side. Cynthia hadn't even been crying herself to sleep at night. She held Jude's hand each time,

watching her daughter's still face. Confused eyes. Waiting for the squeal of excitement - the radiant smile - that would never come. When Samuel didn't toss and turn, the strangest dreams plagued his conscious. All about Jude. Completely normal, apparently. Normal in the oddest sense. According to Harriet, anyway. Watching the weight pile on the bloated young woman, knowing nothing could be done. That was normal? Normal was watching with awe as Jude ran through the house, jumped with excitement at *Fireman Sam* or *Danger Mouse*, or beat someone at snooker. This evening, Cynthia went on her own. Promising to call when anything changed.

At two minutes past midnight, Jude had gone to sleep, one last time.

Seven

Samuel couldn't help Jude. Or Cynthia. If the seizure had never happened, Samuel would never have met Joan. Or the many other people he decided from that moment, that he wanted to try and help. Do what he couldn't do for Cynthia. What he should have done. What he - along with Buckley - could try to do to help this woman by the toilet door. Why didn't he ask Harriet what 'enough' was? In all of the following nights that they spent together, he had never once asked.

Perhaps he could try asking Caroline it again. Or let Buckley deal with it. Deal with someone who was just too far gone. How could Samuel do this? How could he?

Eight

In three days, Helen would be gone. Moylan sighed. Such a shame she couldn't wait until the year was out. Then again, Moylan would be able to eagerly meet her replacement. He hadn't heard much from other staff about them. Not from the few colleagues currently scattered around him in the staffroom. Talking only about their mundane little lives. Even Helen. Obviously Scanlon. Moylan looked at Helen from her pretty face to slender feet. Perhaps Moylan would become reacquainted with a familiar face. Which one, though? Edward Lyons from his younger days? Oh, sweet Edward. Norman Harris? Someone who didn't know about the box. Whoever it would be, Moylan would be waiting, hand outstretched for them to shake. And never mention the box. Scanlon, was he masking his small talk for Moylan's ears, simply waiting

until Moylan left, to then blurt it all out? Spill Moylan's guts everywhere, as messily and loudly as he could?

Just three more days.

Carrying his case in hand, and sports bag over his shoulder, Moylan strolled through the school entrance, quickly glancing at several students sitting or standing along the corridor. For once, the morning traffic rush hadn't bothered him. Perhaps Helen's replacement had been among it. Newly qualified, or quite experienced? Knowing how to keep order, just as Moylan did. Maybe he wouldn't be the first to greet them, but he would be the one to make the best impression. He opened the staffroom door and entered.

Several other colleagues had already had the pleasure, he could see. An older strawberry-blonde woman, in a loose olive dress, with the most sumptuous…oh, such rounded breasts. Moylan placed down his case and bag and began to approach the woman.

'Hello, I'm Peter Moylan. Head of English.'

The woman turned, but didn't exchange Moylan's smile. Her expression was simply…neutral.

'Oh, are you?' she replied. 'Shame that I'm in the Maths department, then. Coleen Harper.'

Moylan smiled, offering his hand, which Coleen graciously accepted.

'Did you get here easily enough, then, Coleen? If not, I'd be happy to give you a lift in the mornings.'

'No, my sister drops me off on her way to her shift at the dry cleaners. Thanks anyway.'

Moylan paused, then eventually nodded.

'Brian also offered. I also declined.'

Moylan smiled. How shrewd.

'If you don't mind, I'd like to…'

Moylan motioned his hand.

'Of course, my dear.'

Coleen turned away. Such a charming woman. A married woman. Moylan returned to

his case and sports bag, taking several glances at the latter. No one would look in there. Not for a shoe box, anyway. Especially not Coleen, whose time would be far too preoccupied with settling in.

Hopefully Coleen would settle in. Maybe she would come around to Moylan, eventually. No. She would. Moylan would make sure of it, now that it seemed unlikely that Scanlon would cheat for the second time - desperation would get him nowhere. Moylan lifted the sports bag and case, one at a time, placing them in his locker. He kept one hand, and his eyes, on the bag. For one minute. Then two. Any longer, and everyone would know.

At last, lunchtime had arrived. Perhaps this time, Moylan would be the first to see the beautiful new woman. Those long locks. All the more to play with. He held his Tupperware bowl, only looking ahead at the staffroom door this time. First one here, he had to be. That free period of marking books hadn't been for nothing. Scanlon's lot before lunch were usually a handful. Oh, yes. Moylan would sit in his usual

spot, awaiting this gorgeous woman's presence. He opened the staffroom door, and-

No one. Just as he suspected. Moylan headed across the room. Perhaps Coleen would-.

'You were never my type, Isaac.'

He stopped midway to his chair. Her voice had come from behind, but Coleen had since made her way to the table facing Moylan. He looked at her, his smile fading to a hardened expression. Watching as she sat down adjacent to his seat.

'Were?'

Coleen nodded.

'And still aren't.'

Moylan kept his eyes on hers.

'Perhaps I ought to wear a name badge around you, Harper,' he said with great disdain. 'It's Peter, not Isaac.'

Coleen smiled.

'So you told me.'

Moylan nodded. Where had that come from? He sat down, opening his Tupperware bowl, containing his usual ham, prawn, and lettuce salad. Isaac? A terrible name. Who would call their boy such a name? Moylan glanced at Coleen, looking through her bag.

'How long have you been running for, then?'

Moylan sniffed, taking out his plastic cutlery.

'Some months.'

'Gavin said you got a new pair of trainers,' Coleen said, still sorting through her bag. 'They Adidas, Nike, or-'

'Nike.'

'What colour? Blue? Green? Or what about pink - nothing wrong with a man being seen in that colour.'

'Black.'

Coleen chuckled.

'Good ol' black.'

Moylan's scowl was fixated on the woman's eyes.

'Quite.'

Moylan moved his hand back and forth on the steering wheel. The shoebox was placed between his feet. Nike; Puma; Adidas. It wouldn't matter in the end. That nosy woman. Ritchie Keenan. Brian Scanlon. Helen. None of them would matter. Not even Coleen Harper. Moylan would make sure of it. Who was that woman to ask those questions? Who was she to even speak to him? Moylan removed the lid of the box. Looking between it and the windscreen. That insufferable bitch.

None of it was going to matter.

Nine

Leonard Glover
Coenway Secondary School
68b Milton Street
Lyffonfeld
GG7 8PO

4th March 1991

Mr and Mrs Cleaver
31 Ashbrook Crescent
Coilston
EL14 5BG

Dear Mr and Mrs Cleaver,

I am writing to inform you that your daughter Caroline will be placed in a period of suspension lasting fourteen days, commencing on 5/3/91 and

ending on 19/3/91. It should be noted that this duration is frankly quite lenient, considering the nature of the incident, and will be subjected to review and extended, if necessary. As I'm sure you will agree, bomb threats/hoaxes are not, and will never be, a laughing matter. I cannot express my disappointment enough, in a student with no previous misdemeanours, who will now possibly be throwing away her future.

If this period of suspension is extended, it is likely to be until her examinations take place. As a result of Caroline's actions and her suspension, she will not be permitted to engage with others, except during break and lunch time.

I hope not to trouble you with a letter of this nature again, at any point in the future. If you wish to discuss any of this letter further with me, please do not hesitate to contact me.

Thank you kindly for your time.

Sincerely,

Leonard Glover,
Principal

Coenway Secondary School
68b Milton Road
Lyffonfeld
GG7 8PO

Ten

5.3.91

It wasn't me! Fucking hell, why would anyone…fuck. Glover picked me because I was the first one he saw. Had to be. What the fuck am I going to do? Mum didn't even shout when she saw it. Dad hasn't come home yet. So, it's all been for nothing. I don't think Glover wants me back. I know it says two weeks, but knowing what Glover's like…

Fuck you, Prat fucking Goss. L might come round later. D definitely will – 'better than sitting bored off my tits in this dump' – if only he had tits. Dad'll blow, won't he? How can I explain to Mum and Dad that it wasn't me? Goss will end up in jail some day, I just know it. Or he'll carry out a bombing for real, hijack a plane and fly it into a skyscraper, or something. Wonder what Audrey thinks of him? Maybe I

could try and see her when I get back. If I get back.

I mean, fucking hell, what if it had happened for real? I wonder if Goss' mates can actually stand him? Bet they know he did this. Not like they'll grass on him. Might go for a walk. Mum couldn't forbid me to do that. It'll be one of a long list of things Dad will ban. So he wouldn't mind if I decided to start eating myself to death?

Would love to see Audrey's yellow coat again. If only I could talk to her, tell her about all of this. Dad wouldn't like her. Maybe I could find a way to see her before she leaves. If I get back, I could. It wasn't for Goss, I could be currently far away from that yapping mutt across the street.

If I don't sleep much tonight, I'll bloody dream about Goss, because I can't stop fucking thinking about him. Might nick Sandra Pritchard's dartboard and stick his face on it. Or an axe. Nah, a face so ridden with holes will do. Am I going to just lie and stare at the cloud outside? Won't make any difference, there'll be

nothing to wake up for. Maybe, all this time, there wasn't. What would Audrey think of my poems? Probably make something out of them that wasn't there. If I can't go for a walk, I might just lie on my bed. Wonder what L and D actually think about the 'bomb threat' hoax? D would want to ask Goss why he's a sick fucking shithead. Two hours and Dad will be home. Fuck.

6.3.91

Hear me out, Glover. You make our lives a misery. I was standing there, waiting on Rachel, and you thought 'I know Goss did it, but I don't care'.

When Mum and Dad have finished their daily shouting round, I will tell them this. I want to tell Audrey it, as well. But fourteen days will become fourteen weeks. I'll tell D when he's over again. L's landline is down.

People aren't interested in the truth. Glover won't resign. He wanted a solution, not the truth. The school will be run into the ground by the time the crown is pried from Glover's cold dead

hands. D reckons Goss will get what's coming to him. Didn't think D was that dense. If I'm allowed back, I will show Audrey my poems. If I get out of bed. If I shower. Mum and Dad have noticed, but none of their shouting has been aimed at me. In fact, they haven't said more than two words to me, since yesterday. They must be as tired as me.

Now she loiters in the derelict street

With pitch black vision

And only half the orange street lights shine bright

On houses that didn't even exist two decades ago

Now she dances like a maniac

With her pitch black vision and frozen hands

Seeing the shadows that linger so vividly

Are they out of their mind, or is everything just a facade?

Is everything really in black and white, or so much more complicated than it seems?

I dream of seeing Audrey. She's not a psychologist, sure, but what would she make of that? If no one else understands, would she? Apparently L tried to call at the house earlier, but parents are having none of it. When D comes, I hope they don't do the same. I might get off my bed, that way.

8.3.91

I don't fucking care. If the shouting stops. If it worsens. Not even about changing my bed sheets. Think I either dreamt or outright hallucinated about L the other day. Her landline's still down. Fucking period has just started. Only got two pads left. I don't even care. Mum's sister, Cherie is coming over tonight, apparently. Don't know why I'm even telling you that, diary. I see my collection of books staring me in the face, which is how I could pass the time tonight. How I could drown out Cherie's shrieks. Even if I don't actually set eyes on her tonight, parents will still force me to scrub up. I wish L's landline was working.

Might cut my hair off. Then I definitely would not be allowed back. Don't think I'd be bothered, anyway.

It's two a.m. Cherie is still here. Isn't it just as well I can't sleep? I wish I could say I can guess what Audrey would think. I've got a name for this poem I wrote - it's definitely apt for what it's about.

Train through an Insomniac's Dreamland

The two of us shared a dream

I sat with her younger self from 1986

Everyone was lonely, even with many of us in the room

My aim in the dark was directionless

All I could hear was her bewildered voice

The darkness faded into blinding royal blue light

At three in the morning, she bit the dissolving dust and welcomed the cold embrace As we sat on a bench, a synthesiser played while the silver sea swooshed about

At five, we strolled down the sepia road painted into the grainy scene

With only another twenty four hours left, we simply stared

When midnight struck, we couldn't remember if there were almost two decades of age between us

Or if the colour of the front door or the car were the same or not

Tiny white dots in the pitch black sky transported us back to 1992

But was it ever really night?

Some said life goes on, but which one, we asked

Our dream or real life?

Though, surely, this is real life

All the colours were reversed, our faces dark instead of light Someday it felt like reality

We did not believe in immortality, but rather the opposite happened, it seemed Forever stayed our current ages, never growing elder

It kept the many lonely people moving along, however

The houses reached their one hundredth year long after the people kicked the bucket

Audrey wouldn't know what to think of that. No one would. Cherie's squeals are doing my fucking head in. If I jumped out of my window out on to the street, none of them would notice. If I got a crew cut, they would not notice. I may try to reread Misery. Or A Clockwork Orange.

10.3.91

If I walk around my room for an hour, do you think – no. D is currently like Mrs Gosford's old dog Copper. He'll catch bits and pieces of your sentences, and that's it. Saw L in the street this morning. And last night. At least I hope I did, and it wasn't a dream. Or in this case, a hallucination. Mum didn't even allow me to make her breakfast, despite it being Mother's

Day. Didn't allow me to offer to do anything for her.

I don't care about Goss, Glover, or any of them, anymore. Maybe if I hadn't been standing where I was, Glover wouldn't have pointed that angry finger at me. Don't think I want to go back. Been too quiet in the house, lately. Maybe Cherie did them a bit of good.

FUCK YOU, GOSS. YOU ABSOLUTE SELF-ABSORBED PRICK.

I will sneak out and go for a walk tonight. Get away from the quiet of this house.

12.3.91

One more week. Maybe I will see Audrey. Even just pass by her office. Didn't stop crying last night. Nothing to do with my period. L hasn't had hers, apparently. Oh no, she has. Fucking lack of sleep. Glover isn't going to let me back, I just know it. Goss will get every accolade going. Strange taste in my mouth. Back is also aching, for some reason.

For real, L's landline is finally getting mended. I know this because she has just been over. Parents are out so finally got catching up for a bit. Didn't find myself actually saying a lot. In fact, half the time we listened to cars passing by outside. If there's something going on with her, she'd have been best telling me.

Phoned L again tonight. Her dad said she was washing her clothes and rearranging her room. Apparently she hasn't said much to D, either. If this is in any way to do with Goss, fuck's sake, L, just tell me. Does she really think I did it? That I have blueprints stuffed in my drawer? What the hell has made her think that? Of the the three of us, D's the biggest trouble maker, but even he knows where to draw the line. Well, I hope so, and that he's not going to turn around tomorrow and reveal himself as the mastermind behind that stunt. If she really thinks I did it, that is her fucking problem.

16.3.91

Spent so long crying through the night. What even for? What even fucking for? Did I even go

*out on my walk. No. Why would I make light of
something like bombs? Has L become paranoid?*

18.3.91

*Maybe it will be all right. Maybe that was
another dream. I'll try again.*

Eleven

Compassionate leave. That would do it. Moylan could go, never to be seen again. It had taken him long enough to decide, since that strange exchange with Coleen Harper three days ago. Three days of avoiding those eyes, taking his tea or lunch elsewhere from the staffroom, or tuning out her soft-as-cotton voice. Once enticing. Now unnerving.

Moylan sat before the principal, Derek Laughlin - a man just as prim and proper as Moylan, wearing his best suit and green tie, as always- in Laughlin's office.

'Sorry to hear about your brother, Peter,' Laughlin said. 'I wouldn't wish his illness on my worst enemy.'

Moylan nodded, clearing his throat.

'It's quite awful, sir.'

Laughlin held a pen between his fingers.

'How long do you think-'

'I'm not sure, sir. Two days might suffice. Then again...'

Laughlin sat back, exchanging Moylan's nod.

'I understand, Peter,' he said. 'My wife lost her fight with it at only thirty-eight.'

Moylan almost felt himself slouching in his chair. Almost...folding his arms. Smiling.

'Back in on Monday, then, sir?'

Laughlin tapped the pen on his desk.

'Yes. But if the worst should happen...'

Moylan nodded.

'Of course, sir.'

He understood, and was glad Laughlin did, too.

Three periods until lunchtime. Hopefully one more lunchtime without having to lay eyes on that woman. Maybe he could retreat to his

room. Mark more books? Sort out his files? Or just sit there and eat. For now, Moylan headed to the staffroom during his free period. It wouldn't have surprised him in the slightest if she was also there. He pushed open the door, allowing a colleague to exit, and entered.

Well. Well. Well.

Coleen was standing at the sink, making herself a cup of tea or coffee, at a guess.

'How's your sister doing?' she asked. 'Better than your 'brother', I take it?'

She headed for her chair. Moylan stepped forward.

'Fine.'

'So, she's at ease, then?'

Moylan looked at her. He turned and began to step away.

'How you've grown, Isaac,' Coleen continued. 'Shame they never did.'

Moylan stopped.

'Have you-'

'Never without your permission.'

Moylan's eyes darted, as he sensed Coleen's smile. She didn't even have to mention it. She knew. Never had Moylan harmed-

It was a long time ago. He had been so desperate to get out. Coleen wouldn't tell Scanlon. Would she? How could she remember? This godforsaken bitch.

Moylan turned around.

'How…did you know what I was going to ask you?'

Smiling, just as he had guessed.

'You keep looking at that sports bag,' Coleen replied. 'Must really be eager for your run.'

Moylan's eyes were fixed on hers. Her ice cold hazel eyes – still the same as when they first met an age ago. Not quite as cold and callous as what she had done.

'Yeah.'

He turned away to the sink. More than a stiff drink was needed.

'She gets out enough these days, then?'

Moylan stopped, then turned. That neutral expression had reappeared.

'I ought to report you, Harper.'

'For what? Something they never could?'

Moylan *was* a coward. As much as he ought to slap this bitch - as much as the rage stewing away inside urged him to - he couldn't. She was being far too nosy about the box. What would 'Isaac' do - this 'Isaac' she insisted on calling him? Ring the bitch's neck - slap her until she was unconscious, like the bitch deserved?

'What is Joan's welfare to you, Harper?'

She chuckled.

'It was going to happen, anyway.'

'What?'

Coleen flashed a smile.

'What?'

Moylan's rage was bubbling, ready to erupt like Pompeii. His hand clenched tight into the edge of the table.

They both turned as the door opened. Gavin bloody Woods.

'Hi, Peter. Coleen,' he chirped. 'Still going for your run this evening, then, Peter?'

'Yes.'

As far away from Coleen Harper, yes. From everyone. Unless...

'You're still welcome to join us on Thursday, if-'

'No. No, thank you.'

Moylan shot a 'don't even' look at Coleen.

Woods nodded, and headed towards his locker. Moylan looked between Coleen and Woods, every painstaking second ticking by. As Woods eventually left, carrying some files, all of Moylan's attention - his frustration, anxiety, and something else he couldn't quite pinpoint - was back on that bitch.

'It was a long time ago.'

If he had gritted his teeth any harder…

Coleen's expression became soft.

'How do you know I know what you're referring to?'

'Why do you keep calling me that name?'

Coleen smiled.

'Just messing,' she replied. 'Shame, though, that they never could.'

Moylan walked towards her. Coleen didn't budge.

'She was always going to go, anyway.'

Moylan paused.

'You said it yourself. Hopeless. Both of them.'

No. No.

Moylan looked at the blonde hair. The slightly ageing skin. The gold ring on her finger. Five years older than him. The ever soft-as-cotton voice.

'Russell.'

Coleen managed a half-smile.

'Isaac.'

How dare she say it like they were old friends.

'Those poor women,' Coleen continued. 'And you just want to run away.'

Moylan stepped away, lifting the sports bag. It felt heavier, but not as heavy as...that thing that everyone had. Apparently. Coleen had buried hers, even deeper than Moylan. For what she had done. The despicable bitch.

As Ethan Anderson read the last line of the current chapter of *Animal Farm*, Moylan found himself staring at the classroom floor, rather than at Mr Fielding's class he had been assigned to cover. Laughlin had only thought it fair to ease him in. Moylan was once again slouched back, with his arms folded. Two weeks. Two weeks of that soft-as-cotton voice playing like a broken record in his mind, but not once seeing her in the flesh. Her voice was enough. Coleen was right,

what could Moylan report her for? He had no evidence, but Coleen… She knew. How could he have forgotten that voice, from all of those years ago?

'Sir?'

Moylan snapped out of his daze, glancing at the class of fourteen before him.

'Very good, Anderson,' he said, smoothly as he could. 'Just continue with your notes, while I excuse myself. Won't be long.'

The boys complied. Moylan headed for the door, and left, shutting it tightly. He continued along to the stairs, and down them until he reached a long corridor - the longest corridor of all corridors in existence. He finally approached the staffroom. Quiet for once. He strode forward, grabbed the sports bag, and as quickly as he had come in, he rushed out.

Moylan walked up the long corridor, the sports bag in hand. No one would know - no one *else* would know. Not even Laughlin. He checked his watch - eight minutes to the next bell. Just enough to fetch his car keys. He

continued along the corridor, until he approached the double doors. Fortunately, no one used Moylan's room on a Friday afternoon.. He just had to grab his car keys. Coleen Russell had somehow never forgotten. About any of it. Coleen was right, though, there hadn't been any hope for his sister. As Moylan reached the top step, he spied the clock above. Six minutes - he could still get away. Could still...

They would know. With Coleen about, they would know. Moylan turned to the top step, still holding the sports bag. They would know. Coleen wou-

Twelve

From the desk of Peter Bernard Moylan:

This is the last time I will write this.

I had to get out. Had to start again. They'd string me up, otherwise. It made me happy. Not, however, that I didn't get to do what I planned, to Joan. I thought I had. But I wouldn't have left the pills out that way. In fact, I wouldn't have used the pills, at all. I know why Coleen did it. Even if I can't prove that she did it. I thought we trusted each other. Well, certainly I trusted her. I told her so much. Yes, I did say that Joan was hopeless. That's why she was seeing a therapist. Coleen remembered everything. I tried to bury that name. Isaac. It really is a wretched middle name. What were my parents thinking? All of those times with Ritchie Keenan, and all of the others, made me happy. I know he hated it, but it made me happy. Coleen only remembered it all

because she kept tabs on me. On my privacy. On every single little thing. I know why she did it. Both things. This is what she wanted. Didn't care about anyone else. Or she wouldn't have got the pills.

All because of it, I had to get away. All because of Cleaver. I only mentioned her name once to Coleen, but that was enough. Cleaver really is hopeless. Thought she would have gone by now. When supervising me, Coleen certainly seemed to know her stuff. Since I won't be able to report her now, you should. She is dangerous and conniving little bitch, who ought not to be allowed near children. Or anyone, for that matter. I know why she did it. Why she took my one last opportunity – my plan - to get rid of that burden in my life. Mr Manson was never going to make her better. Hopefully he knows that. Just like Coleen would never make Cleaver better. Cleaver wouldn't have lasted six days with her. Coleen would do to her, exactly what she did to Joan. Despite christening me with the most abhorrent name, I cannot say that I didn't love my mother and father. I mentioned them briefly

to Coleen in our second session. Unimpressed, the conversation cut back to Cleaver. Always. Some of the other clients got some sort of look in. All because she was keeping tabs about it all.

Do you know how difficult forging those documents were? I really should have picked a different subject to 'study'. Sitting through each day, but thinking 'it will be worth it'. Until I met that bitch again. I enjoyed those times with those boys, as I said. Just wanted to see what it would be like with the opposite sex, after all of those pleasurable times with women. Boys are just that bit more...exciting. Brian Scanlon will be pleased he was right.

I trusted Coleen, but she could be intimidating. It must have rubbed off on me. Only a few could truly look me in the eye. Not even Cleaver. I could only truly look Coleen in the eye, occasionally. How did she find those pills? Take a wild guess why I never informed the police. Why it will always be suicide. Cleaver's parents were intriguing people. I told them what I had to. It's a shame that their daughter allowed them to suffer how they did. Muriel did tell me

all about her date. At least Cleaver offered to pay.

If I had stayed any longer in that job in that office, she might have made a move. Like Scanlon. But not Laughlin. Thanks, Laughlin. Scanlon would have been shouting in an echo chamber. Only about the stuff with the boys, mind you. To both him and Laughlin, I'll always be Peter Moylan.

Coleen Russell (now Harper) made me like this. Since that fateful first day in 1980. That wretched bitch. When I walked into her office for the first time, she insisted I be called 'Isaac'. It was like she knew. She always had a bottle of apple juice. Although, one time it certainly didn't smell like that. I do regret disclosing Cleaver's name to her, but it did just sort of come out. Speaking of such, I'm still disappointed that Cleaver never did. She really was in denial. Coleen was just waiting for the right moment. I feel sorry her husband. No doubt he's the one who gets the black eyes in this marriage. Even at such an age. She asked, in long, explicit, detail, if such an absurd thing had ever occurred with

Cleaver. Only with those boys. In my then soon-emerging middle age, I realised she just meant fantasies.

It felt good. But please, do something about Coleen.

Thirteen

Gillanmore Police Department
Incident Report

Case number: 008634

Date: 05/06/2020

Reporting Officer: Deputy Kyle Sampson

Incident: Workplace Misconduct

Address of Incident:
Sorcroft Boys Grammar School
57 Arden Road
Gillanmore
GE49 LQT

At 1439, I received a call to Sorcroft Boys Grammar School. Upon arrival, the principal Derek Laughlin informed me that a member of

teaching staff discovered a colleague, identified as sixty-four year old Peter Moylan, deceased at the bottom of a staircase, along with a navy Puma sports bag. The complete contents of the bag are to be confirmed, and this report will be updated as appropriate.

Contents of the sports bag were as follows: one shoebox containing a piece of writing by Moylan, and one half-full water bottle. The writing disclosed that Moylan was found to be perpetrating behaviour of a predatory nature towards numerous students, as confirmed by colleague Brian Scanlon. Another colleague Coleen Harper confirmed that Moylan had used extensive fraudulent means to disguise his true identity, history, and misconduct, as therapist Andrew Isaac McNally. The writing appeared to also disclose activity by Harper and Laughlin which warranted further police interest. Both have now been detained for questioning. No resistance of arrest from Harper. The same could not be said for Laughlin. The school will be placed under review.

Fourteen

A last ditch attempt. That's all Samuel could try with Caroline now. She was outright refusing to surrender the gun, hugging it tight against her chest. Like it was her baby. The one she never intended to have, anyway. She hadn't even intended to do this. Whatever it was. When Caroline walked into Andrew McNally's office for the first time, all of those years ago, none of what had been happening in here today, once crossed her mind as even a remote possibility. Why would it have? How many days before today, had Caroline waited for Samuel to turn up? Someone like him. Someone better. Someone better than McNally, anyway. Marching around with that gun in here, just waiting.

'No. You can't have it, Andrew.'

Samuel looked at the woman, tears

streaming down her red face, as if she had been screaming.

'Andrew doesn't want it,' he replied, longing for Caroline to look at him. 'He wouldn't have any use for it.'

Caroline shook her head.

'You're wrong.'

'Don't-'

Caroline shot up, standing to her full height.

'I won't.'

Samuel nodded. He didn't know what else to do.

'You can't have it, Andrew,' Caroline continued.

Her hand flexed around the handle.

'Why can't Samuel have the gun, Caroline?'

Samuel looked to the door, as Buckley spoke. Then back at Caroline, who-

'Caroline-'

BANG!

Fifteen

26/5/1995

God. Forgot all about this. Been too busy to remember to write in it, obviously. My supervisor, George, has been egging me on to go for the promotion. His deputy. Why not? Never short of a laugh in that place, even if it is a stationary shop. It's great, really. Madge is arranging a night out (just dinner in that new place down the road), for Tuesday. Her blonde hair suits her – I mean it when I say it takes about five years off her. I love how she calls everything 'beautiful', 'gorgeous', or 'lovely'. Dad's new car is great - he's even offering to take me to work on Thursdays. D's coming round tomorrow - looking forward to it.

To be continued…

Printed in Great Britain
by Amazon